HOPE OF THE WORLD

THE WORLD BURNS BOOK 11

BOYD CRAVEN III

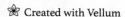 Created with Vellum

1

"So, Michael," Shannon said, taking his hand, "tell me, where are you from exactly? You don't sound like you're from this part of the world."

"Alabama, ma'am," Michael said, trying not to get tongue tied around the older and very beautiful DHS woman.

"You don't have to call me ma'am... Aren't you going to ask me where I'm from?" she said, stopping.

They were both between the rows of APCs, one row off from where Michael had parked their rolling Russian rust.

"Where are you from, Shannon?" Michael asked, feeling like a piece of sandpaper who was trying to be smooth.

"Canton Texas, though I went to school up in North Dakota," she said, giving his hand a squeeze.

"I'm sorry if I suck at talking to people, I'm not used to this..."

"Do I scare you?" Shannon asked him, turning to face him.

"A little bit," Michael told her truthfully.

"You're twice my size, came in here wearing two guns

like you know how to use them both, and you're afraid of me?" she asked, her lips curving up into a smile.

"Not afraid, ma'am, just a little scared," Michael admitted. "You're just so pretty, every sane thought just flies straight out of my head when you're close by."

"Well then, maybe this can help."

Shannon pulled him close and kissed him deeply. Michael was almost too startled at first, but he quickly returned the passion. After a few more seconds, they both pulled away.

"Wow," Shannon said, flushed and a little bit breathless.

"Wow is right," Michael agreed. "So, I don't have any college education, I actually didn't even graduate high school."

Shannon looked at him surprised, and he started to walk, his hand still linked with hers. She followed, instead of breaking the grip, as Michael led her slowly toward the APC.

"WHAT'S THE PLAN?" KING ASKED.

"We've got three minutes and forty-five seconds before the HVAC is going to go on the fritz and start venting diesel exhaust from the backup generator. Then the servers are going to open every door and prevent the electronic locks from working. Once the internal sensors show that evacuation has been completed, the computers are going to wipe themselves. This will then effectively become a big, fortified hole in the ground with a big wide open front door," Caitlin said, her accent muted as she stated the facts in a clinical tone.

"Good. Bad guys?"

Caitlin sniffed. "Sugar, trust me, those Jihadis won't be an issue, nor anybody who dined with them, and as long as Smith's got his end all figured out, he should have gotten my coded signal."

"Do you really think we'll be able to get all the turncoats outside?" John asked, "or is it one of those 'get out or die' situations?"

"Hon, unless they got oxygen tanks, they're gonna want to vent this puppy out. It'll be an hour before they can fix what I did *IF* the computers were online. They won't be. They can manually kill the genny, but that's on the bottom of four, where all the exhaust will be the worst. My best guess is that it'll be a turkey shoot. Smith's men should be ready with the heavy stuff with the rest of the Kentucky Mafia ready to capture or kill."

"Good, so we'll be ready with our APC to take out the other armor as needed. Who's staying out to call the shots if we need artillery?"

"That would be me," Tex said sardonically, "but you already know that you're the one who said I can't move my ass fast enough."

"Oh yeah, that's right..." John said with a grin, and gathered everything he'd been collecting.

Tex and John had talked with King's 'door key', and they'd taken back some of the gear and supplies they had walked out of the APC with, so they wouldn't be disarmed when the S hit the F. John looked left to right and then passed out articles of sweats from an oversized duffel that had bulky objects wrapped inside of them.

"Time?" King asked.

"Any second—"

Loud klaxons went off, and everyone in John's group took a deep breath, wondering if they would be able to

3

smell the exhaust right off. The alarm was loud and deafening. Some people who were still in uniform ran toward the large blast doors, but most people milled about in confusion. It was easy to see who had been based here and in the know, and who were the NATO and uncompromised units. In the mass of confusion, everyone in the group was going to sneak out. At least that was the plan.

"Go," he said, looking at the group.

"Let's do it, ladies," Tex said, jumping up wincing and holding his right butt cheek.

Four of the core group got together with the rest of the Kentucky Mafia, as they'd started to call themselves, and headed for the exit a little ahead of everyone else. Once people saw that they were starting an actual evacuation and that it was a fire drill or real-life fire, they moved too. That was when the smoke from the diesel exhaust got piped throughout the top level. All hell broke loose, and people started to cough and shout and yell. John looked up and easily found the flashing red lights over the large blast door.

"This way, guys," John said, directing everyone. "Everyone knows their job, let's get ready to do this."

"You, you got this. We just have to make sure that Michael ain't got stuck with some young thing," Caitlin said with a grin.

"That boy is going to die a virgin," King said, smiling.

"I'm that kid's godfather," John said with a snarl. "He's been a little boy ever since I've known him, he's been a little bit of an older boy even now, but until I can get a hold of his mom and dad, he's still a little boy. Do you understand me?" John wasn't smiling.

Everyone had a good chuckle at that, and they started out with the rest of everyone else. All the new people from the NATO had irregular GHS units crashing at the same site; it was mass chaos. No one had planned for this number of people, they hadn't put together any drills for this number of people, and it showed.

Before running out into the parking area with APCs haphazardly parked in rows, John's group immediately headed toward their APC, with Tex stopping just a little bit away. Caitlin passed him a handheld radio, and Tex put in the earwig and clipped on the push to talk button and fired it up. He immediately talked to Sgt. Smith, but his words were lost in the crowd of people that were rushing through.

"Michael, what the hell is going on?" Shannon asked as the alarm sounded.

"God, that sounds like the fire alarm to me," Michael said, unsurprised.

"I'm not here with my regular people, what are we supposed to do?" Shannon asked him, her dark hair blowing in the wind.

Michael felt conflicted about Shannon, and he was torn. To tell her the truth, or to risk finding out that she was in on everything else? Never before had Cupid shot him, but he'd shot him good this time. His biggest worry was that he'd got shot right in the ass. He thought about it for half a second and then motioned her toward the back of APC and opened the door.

"Shannon, what do you know about this place?" Michael asked quietly, barely overheard over the klaxon of the fire alarm.

"Not much, I just know that we were told to stand down and to come back to this location."

"What was your job before you guys were told to come up here?"

Shannon looked at him thoughtfully for a second, knowing that he had something else on his mind. "You're getting around to something, aren't you?"

"I'm not actually with the DHS," Michael admitted. "I've been sent here to infiltrate this facility to gauge the involvement of the New Caliphate within branches of our own government."

Michael stood there for a moment as his words hit Shannon like a bombshell. The horror on her face was almost immediate.

"You mean, that the DHS... That can't be true," Shannon protested angrily.

"We've got all the proof we need now," Michael told her, "we're the ones who pulled the fire alarm."

"So, you coming out here with me... You mean you were just using me as a... I'm your diversion to get outside?" she snapped before letting one manicured hand fly and slapping him on the cheek.

"I'm sorry," Michael said.

"Are you making this up?" Shannon asked, her voice quiet despite the chaos erupting behind them.

"No, it's the absolute truth. I'm with what people are starting to call the United States militia, otherwise known as the Kentucky Mafia."

"You mean like Blake Jackson? Like the guy from Rebel Radio and his wife, Sandra?" Shannon asked, flexing her hand to get the pain out.

"The very same. I don't know how much you've been aware of, but I need to know where you were, what you used to do for the DHS."

"I was working in northern Texas, attached to an ICE

contingent watching for drug runners cutting through New Mexico and Texas," Shannon said angrily.

Michael watched her face and saw the way she'd reacted to the question, and he knew that she was probably telling him the truth. For now, he would trust, but verify. How he planned on doing that was anybody's guess. But if he could make her a friendly... Michael shook his head. He was thinking like an agent; he wanted to help Shannon out as more than just an asset. She was probably the first person that he'd ever found who had totally blown his socks off.

"Pretty soon here friends are going to be showing up and if you're not with the Jihadis—"

"Michael fired it up," John yelled over the shouting people who were starting to swarm the parking lot.

Michael looked around, and Shannon looked in the direction John's voice had come from. A large group of the Kentucky Mafia was moving through the crowd, headed straight for the APC. Michael jumped inside and held his hand out to Shannon. "Are you with us, or are you with the Jihadis?"

"I'm with the United States of America," Shannon said haughtily.

"You get your ass in, sugar," Caitlin said, already pushing the younger woman.

2
———

"**K**halid," Hassan said, rushing into the command post, "radio contact in the DHS facility has gone silent."

"My dear cousin, why is this unusual?" Khalid said.

"Because I've been unable to reach those loyal with us within the DHS," Hassan said, wiping sweat from his brow.

"Cousin, you were the director of the Department of Homeland Security, you know all about these facilities. Tell me... what is it that you're worried about?"

"I am worried that our people have been compromised, captured, or killed. It was very convenient that several days ago two facilities were attacked nearby and there was a lot of new DHS who were assigned to the area to flee there."

"So what you're telling me, is that somehow the facility was breached?" Khalid asked his cousin.

"That is the worst case scenario, cousin."

Khalid looked at his cousin thoughtfully for a moment, before starting to pace the lobby of the Motel 6 they'd taken as a command post. They were waiting for their agents to escape with the codes needed to disable and gain access to the nuclear facilities where the Air Force was held.

"Hassan, what is our backup plan if we don't get those codes?"

"There is no backup plan," Hassan said. "This is the only DHS facility where I had access to the Air Force's mainframes remotely. That's why it is where it is. This used to be an Air Force facility, part of the continuation of operations. I still had access, because not everything was decommissioned before I had this bunker renovated and upgraded. The men that were stationed there were my men, and the fact I can't get them on the radio, or even secure other secure channels, has me very concerned."

Khalid started to pace even faster, and his face turned an alarming shade of red.

"Our advisors from North Korea are starting to defect, our supply chains coming from Mexico in the boats has now been completely cut off, been sank or requisitioned by the cartels or stolen by the American government. Our own men, the men you recruited to our cause, are still with us. For now."

Hassan looked at his cousin, and after a few moments nodded his head.

"So we are stuck in the middle of the country with no supplies, no resupply, and no way out?"

"This is the way it's always been, cousin. I've been here myself for twenty-five years, helping to plan this operation. You know the sacrifices that must be made in the name of Allah. Please, cousin, don't lose faith now."

Khalid looked at him in surprise. "Faith? You talk to me of faith? You don't even know the word faith. I've been doing the work of the Imams for three years, and I have not one shred of faith!" Khalid screamed. "I've been running on faith and conviction in the movement and the cause, and the abilities of the men around us, and in the plan. You tell me to have faith in Allah? You really think he cares that we're stuck in a nation that hates us and wants to kill us?"

Hassan looked at his cousin in shock; he'd always thought his cousin was a very thoughtful and religious person. It was how he'd got up through the ranks, how even the hard-core Salafists had accepted the meteor-like rising of Khalid through the ranks of the New Caliphate, winning one battle after another across Africa and parts of the Middle East.

"If our people could defeat the Americans and Russians in Afghanistan and Pakistan, what is a country that does not know how to fight and survive in the old ways?" Hassan asked, "Khalid, we've already crippled or killed nine out of every ten infidels. Even if my men are dead and the plan for the nuclear bases is compromised, there is still hope for us. You may not have faith in Allah, but I do."

Khalid stopped pacing and looked at his cousin. A few moments ago he had been nervous and scared to share the potentially bad news. It was definitely not something they had ever thought possible while devising the plan, but if they lost the ability to cut the fangs off the American beast, it might come back to bite them. Fatally, even, if the news from North Korea was any indication.

"Tell me, Hassan," Khalid said softly, "if the base is compromised and an enemy force is occupying it, how many men would it take to retake it and get the codes out?"

Hassan thought for a moment.

3

"Patrick," the president said into his intercom.

"Yes, Mr. President?" he asked, walking through the doorway that the Secret Service was guarding.

"Oh, there you are. I thought I had made myself clear that Col. Grady was to be kept under house arrest?"

"He was, sir."

"Was?" the president asked. "Then where is he now, and where are the men who were assigned to watch him until we could have his trial?"

"Sir... They defected."

"Defected, Patrick?"

"Apparently, the good Col. had even more friends than we could have anticipated. Not only did he have several air drops coordinated in the vicinity of the Homestead, but he also had air drops sending out anti-aircraft materials and materials dropped out west where they had a contingent of regulars waiting to reinforce what they are now calling the Kentucky Mafia, or the United States Militia. I believe it was through Col. Grady and Sandra that the small state militias started to band together, and it's my belief that they, and friends within this own government, have helped him escape."

"To where?" the president demanded.

"Sir, I wish I knew. I would tell you, but I don't think I have anything other than guesses. I think he quite literally said something like 'hunt a hole.' The way he and the team that helped him escape vanished, I think it's likely that they are somewhere nearby. Maybe in one of the old decommissioned cold war bunkers scattered throughout the mountains here."

"He wouldn't stay close. That's too obvious a place to look. What about my appointment for his replacement?" the president asked.

"Well, sir... we're still working on getting the house and senate back together, but the communication issues have been insurmountable thus far. We're lucky the Supreme Court didn't lose all members with that low-yield nuclear device. As you know, only two of them were attending when it went up."

"Are you forgetting that Martial Law is in effect?" the president asked his oldest friend and aid.

"No, sir, but it would make the legitimacy of the replacement—"

"Why wouldn't it be legitimate?" the president asked Patrick.

"I'm not saying it wouldn't be... but public perception is that—"

"You know what? I'm signing an EO, and I want Malik Jefferson sworn in immediately."

"Yes, Mister President," Patrick said, backing out of the room slowly.

"I'm sick of all this right-wing suspicion that's going around," he muttered when he was alone, before holding both hands over his eyes and resting his elbows on the desk. "I'm tired of all these clingers..." he said, and then in a deeper, mocking tone, "My God, my guns, my glory—"

A door opened, and the Secret Service rushed in shouting. He had been about to stand up to pace, a habit he'd done often lately, especially now that he'd been out of the bunker.

"Sir, we need to move you now," one black suited, sunglass wearing, earwigged agent yelled, rushing toward him.

"What's going on?"

Another agent reached the president half a step ahead of the first. He tried to loop an arm under the president to pull him, and that was when the explosion rocked the office. It vaporized everyone within a thirty-foot radius, and the debris from the blast would go on to kill another seven and wounding dozens. The second explosion was triggered half a heartbeat later, closer to the president's secret elevator for times of attack and crisis. Nobody was close enough to be killed by the blast, but that was only because they were already dead.

"Do you got him?" one agent screamed.

"Got him, found the detonator in his hand," another screamed back.

"Patrick, why? You were the president's closest friend!" a secret service agent asked.

""Sic semper evello mortem tyrannis," Patrick panted, as he was roughly cuffed by a man he'd known for half his professional life.

"What?" the agent said, the heat from the spreading fire making him sweat.

"Sic semper tyrannis, thus I always bring death to tyrants," Patrick replied as he was hauled to his feet.

The agent was beyond his breaking point, and the Latin he should have known from his Catholic upbringing and service record had fled him. He'd witnessed a man whom he'd invited to his daughter's baptism party, pull out a chromed detonator and assassinate the President of the United States. He drew his service weapon and pressed the barrel into Patrick's now closed right eye.

"Why?" the agent all but sobbed.

"To prevent a nuclear holocaust," Patrick said.

"Somebody... Who..."

"There's no one left for the order of succession," the agent said, a thought that had been haunting him for a long time, "they were all killed in the nuke."

"And I just stopped China from doing the same to us, so I made a deal," Patrick explained. "Take the cuffs off and make it look like I was trying to get away. I don't want any of my family to suffer through a trial."

The agent didn't hesitate, but nor did he remove the cuffs.

4

"... Say again. Over?" Grady said into the microphone of an old radio set that looked like it had been last used during WWI.

"The President has been assassinated, and his assistant, Patrick, was found with the detonator. He was killed trying to escape. The Air Force is already on high alert because of the New Caliphate's efforts to breach various nuclear facilities, but now we've got reports of Chinese bombers inbound with heavy escort. Over."

"I was afraid that's what you were going to say. Over," the retired Col. told the radioman.

"Sir, the order of succession has been... over."

"I know, son. I'm still in an undisclosed location with men who our former president would consider traitors due to their leaving his administration the way they did. What would you have me do? Over."

"Sir, we formerly request you to make yourself available during this crisis."

"I upheld my oath, to the very letter. I made that rabble-rousing, community organizer fire me by telling him the truth. I am not turning myself in to be convicted by a kangaroo court—"

"Sir," the young airman said, talking over his signal, "you are not being asked to turn yourself in to be tried."

"Excuse me? Over?"

"Sir, we need you."

Grady was silent a moment, still trying to digest what they were asking of him. "I was removed from my position. Over."

"Martial Law is still in effect, the constitution has been suspended. We need somebody to finish carrying us through this crisis until new elections can be held. Over."

"Give me an hour, and I'll be back on the radio. Over."

"Yes, sir. Over and out."

Grady handed the handset back to the man who'd defected with him to run the dials and switches that were augmented with newer coms gear, capable of allowing them to speak on secured channels.

"Do you think this is legit?" his radio operator asked, a hopeful note in his voice.

"The guy on the other end of that conversation is one of two people still over on the other side who I'd trust with my life. Both of his sons served with me over the course of their careers. He would have given a signal if he was compromised and giving bad information. So yeah, it looks like we may not have to stay in hiding any more."

"What do we do now?" the radio operator asked him.

"We wait. I need to walk a bit and think. This is a lot to take in all at once."

"Yes, sir."

Col. Grady left the coms shack, which was really just a concrete room that had been poured in place. The entire complex they were in was an old abandoned copper mine from the early 1900's. The old mining techniques had left the land a blighted area, and the government had taken control and had been making token efforts to clean up the biological disaster before more regulations had been put in place because of bad past practices.

Using the guise in WWII and during the cold war of the Reagan years, the entire complex had been built and fortified. Modern engineering had constructed it the first time, and it had been updated in the eighties. It had been mothballed at the turn of the millennia. And in the last few months, Col. Grady had started the process of bringing the old base back online. It wasn't hard to funnel supplies and work through continuity of operations' executive order that had already been written.

Grady had been very careful, though, he only had his own people; people who were known, worked with, served with, who he'd entrusted with his life in on the project. There'd been warnings that North Korea, operating in accordance with the Jihadi group now known as the New Caliphate, had been planning something major. The president of the United States had been briefed about all of it, but he'd refused to look at the problems from radical Islamic terrorism that faced him. His failure, more than anything else, had led to the destruction and death of millions of American people. That was what Col. Grady had been fearing, and hearing that the president had been assassinated came as a shock... But only shock that it had taken so long to happen.

Suspicions regarding his Department of Homeland Security chief had been circulating for a while, but the president would hear nothing of it. His crony capitalism and political appointments made him a laughing stock of the area. Davis, otherwise known as Boss Hog, had been one such appointment. The president had been gunning for a while for Malik Jefferson, another Harvard law friend, to a post high in his administration. The latest CIA dossier on Malik Jefferson showed someone with a far left progressive liberal ideology that bordered on flat out socialism or even communism.

Now, everything was gone. It was all undone. High-ranking military commanders were left holding the strings, and Grady thought about how he could've been one of them. Hell, he *was* one of them, according to them; they wanted him to come back in. Grady swiped a key card access as he was walking toward the back of the base, and the door slid open. Grady stepped through and waited for the door to close behind him. The rock wall led deeper into the copper mine, and work lights were strung along the ceiling, here and there. It was access to the deeper portion of this mind, and there was, at one point, an estimated 450 miles' worth of tunnel dug in just this area alone, not necessarily just this one mine.

Grady had often come down here to walk and think, and that's what he needed to do right now. The man who'd called him had been someone that he trusted implicitly. If the president was really dead, and there was no order of succession to follow at this point, then they really were looking for a leader to step up and do things. Grady knew that, because of the loyalty of his men and the respect from his fellow generals and colonels in the Armed Forces, he might be the natural choice. It seemed that was what the case was here, but he wasn't sure he wanted the job.

He thought about how the political structure of the United States had changed over the years. Serving one's country, it used to be about doing something for other people. Now acting in the capacity of the leader of the free world cost money to get in, and there was even more of a monetary reward when you left. Speeches could be had for half a million dollars a shot, criminal indiscretions were swept under the rug, and lawsuits were quietly settled by super PACs. It used to be the House and Senate, and presidents were men of means who could afford to take some time off to come and serve, but Grady scratched his head trying to remember when career politicians became the norm.

If this was the actual case, then if he served... he mused... he would only do so until legal elections could be held. He paced the tunnels, the floors well-worn from the passage of hundreds of thousands of footsteps over the years. By the time he made it back to the blast door leading to the back of the bunker, he had made up his mind. He would do it, but he'd set a timeframe on it: just time enough to make sure the country didn't fall apart with every governor trying to seize control of power for themselves in every state. Grady swiped his pass card and entered the bunker, and headed immediately to the radio communication shack.

"Felix, I want you to open a channel to Sandra Jackson."

"Yes, sir!" Lieut. Felix said, as he put his headphones on squarely and twisted the dials and pushed buttons.

5

The man formerly known as Dick Pershing, but who now went by his real name, Mike, and his best friend and companion, Courtney, were making a wide loop into the extreme eastern side of Texas in their looted Hummer. Their plan was to travel down toward Houston, where some of the cartels had been trying to ferry the Jihadis. Courtney was monitoring the radio transmissions when the news broke that much of their Navy and transport ships had been bombed by the US Air Force.

It wasn't long before they decided that it was time to start heading west, where the main thrust of the cartels had been trying to keep the supply lines open between the Jihadis and the bulk of the troops. Mike laughed at himself; he hadn't realized that, while he was being interrogated by Skinner, so much had been going on. It was one thing to hear about it on the radio, but he had no idea they were so close. The day they headed west, they heard about the U.S. Navy torpedoing ships on the West Coast that were working with the cartels. Rumors also claimed that some of the ships and submarines that were engaging the US military were of Korean nature.

One wild theory, started by someone who claimed to have worked for the President's secretary, said that the United States had nuked North Korea out of existence and that the Chinese were coming to attack. Mike needed a fight, and Courtney was itching to get into the action again herself. It was almost strange; as Mike left the shell of Dick Pershing behind, Courtney's dreams and nightmares started manifesting and affecting her. For so long she'd stayed strong to keep Dick together to get home to see Mary and Maggie, and now her subconscious needed time to rest and heal as well.

Still reeling from the loss of her soon-to-be husband, and her own symptoms of PTSD from all the rape and torture, she was fine when she was awake. She told Mike on more than one occasion that for every invader she killed, she felt a small measure of relief. It was one less person to kill one of the United States citizens - fathers, mothers, daughters, teachers, cousins, and friends. They weren't a couple, but they were the closest thing to platonic friends that a man and a woman could be. There had been one time when Mike thought he was Dick and he mistook Courtney for who he thought his wife was, Mary; it had been a confusing situation for everyone all around.

"Dick... I'm sorry I mean Mike, we've got some guy named King on the radio, and it keeps fading in and out. Is that the same guy you asked me to listen for?" Courtney asked.

"Don't worry about getting my name messed up, I still do it all the time too. When you live as another man for so long, it changes you. You start fitting into their personality, but I think right now part of me needs to be both Mike *and*

Dick. And yes, King, I do need to get in touch with him. I was given some real basic frequencies to monitor for him, but when he goes to the ultra-secret scramble stuff, we don't have a prayer of communicating with them."

"I know, the weather must be just right, because it sounds like they are raising hell in Nebraska of all places." Courtney almost had to shout over the noise of the wind.

It was turning late fall, and it was still hot in Texas. What some Texans would call the weather turning cool was still a good 75 to 80F during the daytime. They had been siphoning fuel, but they had also brought along a small generator that Mary's father had given them. Before leaving the family compound in Arkansas where Mary and Maggie were, Mike had helped the old man and Mary fortify their homestead a little bit more. He didn't worry too much because the old man might've been mean and angry, but it was Maggie's grandma, Mary's mother, who was the real hell on wheels. Dick wanted to make sure that he left the homestead well protected because part of him knew that, in order to heal, he needed to get out of there now that it was safe for him to travel again.

He'd come apart at the seams and completely lost out on who he was. PTSD sucked, but that wasn't the only thing Mike had been dealing with, and so many memories had been repressed. Clean, sober, and back in his element, Mike, the Devil Dog, was ready to go to war. He listened as Courtney tried transmitting.

"Dick, I've got a response here, but it's not King. It's someone who is with King, a guy named Michael, and also John, Tex, and Caitlin. Do any of those names mean anything to you?" Courtney asked.

"You know, you just said the name John. Ask him if it's John Norton."

Courtney did, and she held the headphones even closer, pressing them tight against her ears.

"Yes, we have John Norton on the radio here, he's asking us to verify who we are."

Mike looked at the road around them and saw the other the stalled vehicles were empty. It appeared to be clear. He pulled right into the center of the median that was slightly elevated and rolled to a stop before putting the Hummer in neutral and turning it off.

"Let me talk," Mike said, making a gimme motion for the headset.

"John Norton, my name's Mike. I served with you on two missions in Afghanistan, and it was your team that rescued me from the bank in Fallujah when my friend Dick Pershing was killed in an ambush. Over."

"If you're the Mike I remember, who's my favorite author? Over."

"My brain's a little fried, but it's not that fried. Robert Frost, good friends make good neighbors, over," Mike said, without missing a beat.

"How is it that you're on a semi-secure radio right now, Mike? Over."

"I sorta liberated some gear, right after someone mistook me for you and decided to play pincushion with me. Over."

"Well Mike, I'm short on time here, and I've got about 300 prisoners to deal with and sort through. Are you joining in the fight? Or are you just reconnecting with old friends to get a knitting circle going? Over."

Courtney snorted, and Mike grinned. With the Hummer stopped, there was no wind noise, no rumbling of the engine... And everything that John Norton had been saying over the radio was easily heard by the woman sitting right next to him.

"I've been told I make some really killer socks, over."

"I'm sorry you got caught up in this mess, Mike. I heard a rumor that the DHS thought they'd captured me, guessing that was you? Over," John asked.

"Yeah, they got me and shot me up full of stuff and played a little slap game with me. Nothing too horrible, not like the mess I got myself into a time or two. Listen, I'm on the horn here with you because we were headed toward Houston, but we got word that everything the cartels were doing there has been blown to hell and back. My next goal is to head toward El Paso. I don't have up-to-date intelligence, but I've heard the cartels are trying to get the supply chain going again. Over."

"Mike, I've got some coordinates I'm going to read off to you. You have a way of following GPS coordinates right now? Over," John asked.

"Yes, I do. The old-fashioned way with the map and a ruler. Over."

"Oh, well yeah, I guess it works. I can have a team down there meet up with you, and they're gonna get you outfitted with proper gear. I can't discuss anything sensitive over an open line. If you're down there about to do what I think you're about to do, then you're going to need all the info and support you can get. Over."

Mike was about to answer when another voice broke in on the transmission. "Mike, that you?"

Mike knew that voice; it was the voice of the enormous black man who had trained him on explosives and unconventional warfare. Dick had already been a lethal soldier and special forces operator, and King had been a force multiplier to everyone who graduated from his personal one-on-one school. Mike had known about Sandra, his protégé, but she had already been in the field when Mike had gone to King for training. King had a voice like two boulders rubbing together, a deep rumbling sound. The man knew that just his size alone intimidated people, and he used as few words as possible.

"You got it, war daddy," Mike said with a grin.

"You watch your mouth, boy, or I'll assign you more PT, over," King said with a hint of anger.

"You still in shape, old man? Over," Mike said with a sardonic grin that wasn't being returned by Courtney.

She was actually looking a little green around the gills over Mike's teasing the big man.

"I've slimmed down some, did a lot for my mobility. You come play, I'll show you," King replied.

Another voice broke into the transmission, "...you don't want to test him, I'm 18 now, and his idea of PT leaves me sore and hurting for a week. Over."

"Ok, I'll get on the horn here, and maybe me and the old man can catch up some other time. My partner in crime is ready to get the coordinates when you're ready to read them off. Over."

Courtney looked around and, found a pen, and held up the palm of her hand. Dick was listening and pulled out a folded map from a pouch on his left hip and handed it to her. She unfolded it just as John's voice came through the speakers. She quickly wrote down the GPS coordinates in the margins and, when John signed off, so did Mike.

"Now what?" she asked.

Mike grunted and took the map.

"Most people have forgotten how to do this. Without fancy equipment, most folks have no clue what the numbers on the bottom and sides of the maps mean," he told her.

"Well, now that you mention it, it's common sense,"

Courtney said and then leaned into Mike in a brief contact of comfort.

"It's not common sense, it's old school, and I'm starting to feel my age," Mike told her, searching around the Hummer for some sort of straight edge.

"It can't be that old school, you're not that much older than me," she snarked.

"I'm older enough to know better, but young enough to keep on going," he told her with a grin.

"That makes no sense, Grandpa."

"You want to walk?" Mike teased back.

"No, because from eyeballing this, we have most of a day's drive to get to where we're going. Look," she said and traced the longitude line with one finger and the lat with the other.

A straight edge would have made the job helpful, but as soon as she started tracing it with her fingers, Mike saw right away where they were going to go, and it was going to take them all of a day, maybe more, to get near El Paso, the direction they were headed in. They would stop outside of a large city somewhere and get a map with a better breakdown of the state and fine tune the GPS coordinates when they got close. John hadn't given them any radio frequencies to contact their men there, but he was sure John would be sending advanced word via secure comms to let them know that Mike and Courtney were on their way.

"My turn to drive," Courtney said.

"Like that went so well last time," Mike sniped back, but he was already opening his door.

6

"How do we separate who is working against the US government and who is blameless?" Stu asked John.

"We have the files," John said, pointing to Caitlin who patted her pocket where a USB drive rested.

"But you'd need a computer?" Stu asked again.

"Bingo," Michael told him, pulling a military Toughbook that he'd liberated from one of the DHS APCs out of his backpack.

They had been holding the men in the top level of the bunker after Caitlin had got into a pressurized suit and gone down to the fourth floor and fixed the venting issue. She'd also got some of the government computers functioning from hard drive images stored on offline tapes. She hadn't got everything back online, just the communications and the door/elevator access control. Right now, the only ones with access were Sgt. Smith's men and the Kentucky Mafia. Well, and Shannon, but that was because when she wasn't fighting with Michael, she was his close shadow, listening in on everything that had been going on.

"What we need to do is figure out who we can trust, and that would make the rest of the work easier as we vet these men and women," Smith said, his fork going in and out of an MRE packet as he chowed down.

"The first level is cramped. I know we have all the normal base men separated and cuffed, but it's been a couple of days, and the men here are growing tired of constantly watching the people and staying in a heightened alert of readiness. If we had more help..."

"You know," Shannon said, "My CO is a pretty good guy. I don't think he'd ever be involved with any of this. If you checked his name first... Well... he has the respect of a lot of men. If we could get a leader like him on our side helping..."

"Give me his name, sugar," Caitlin said, already booting up the Toughbook and pulling the USB drive from her pants pocket, "spell it out for me."

"Barnes, B A R N E S," she said, "Clayton Barnes."

"Okay, easy enough. He's not on the list. Actually, your entire group isn't on the list."

"That's what I've been telling you guys," Shannon said indignantly.

"Trust but verify," King rumbled.

Shannon stepped back from the big man who'd gone back to his normal combat comfort wear, black pants and his tactical vest. How not having a shirt on and the vest not chafing the big man was anybody's guess, but Michael had been with King for months and months now, almost as long as he'd spent in the national forest with John and the kids, and this attire was his norm.

"Shannon, will you go collect your CO? If anybody gives you problems, refer them to King or me."

"Yes, sir," she said and snapped off a salute – and nobody was quite sure if it was given with sarcasm or a hint of irony.

Michael watched her leave and swore she made her hips sway a bit as he watched. He was about to ask why suddenly everybody was snickering at him when Shannon turned around and dropped him a wink. Busted, he turned around to see King grinning.

"May not have gotten you away from Kentucky fast enough," he said in a rare display of words.

"I'm not getting hitched and having babies," Michael shot back, "I just met her."

"I just got together with Tex a couple months back, and we're getting hitched and having a baby," Caitlin said with a sardonic grin.

"Guys..."

"Hey, you roll with the punches," John said, liking how the kid still acted like a kid, "otherwise you're not grown up enough to be... well..."

Michael was standing facing John and saw a blur of movement as somebody in sweats rushed at John from behind. Actually, almost everybody but Smith had been facing the young warrior when the DHS turncoat hiding in plain sight made his move. He was one of the volunteers who'd been working on getting food and water for everybody with help from the kitchen. In his hands he had a butcher knife, and was within ten feet of John's back when Michael made his move.

The young man had kept his father's matching set of Colts, and in his first gunfight, he'd shot several corrupt cops in the vests squarely. The cops had been stealing supplies and vehicles from survivors, and when they'd tried to strong-arm Michael and John, Michael had found out he had the gift of shooting naturally ingrained in him. The guns just felt right in his hands, almost like an extension of his fingers. He could also draw and fire them fast, not quite as fast as a cowboy in a spaghetti western, but faster than most men.

John saw Michael's hands blur as the kid made an impossibly fast draw with both guns and dropped just as the knife was swinging down at his back in an overhand strike. He trusted Michael, and he knew if he was fast enough, the best thing he could do was clear the way for Michael to have a clean shot to whatever danger he'd seen.

King also registered the problem as the kid made his move. He half turned, seeing Michael using his natural talent, and was horrified to find he wasn't going to be fast enough to help him out. Caitlin, Tex, and Smith were caught flat footed and jerked in surprise when John flopped, but Michael fired four times. He hit twice in the chest, once to the throat and once in the forehead of the knife-wielding man. The man's momentum kept him going and, instead of the knife plunging down into John's back, he tripped on John's dropping form and went over the top, the knife clattering to the ground inches from his left eye.

John rolled, and the corpse kept moving, almost embracing him with a wet sticky trail. He got to his knees slowly as Michael kept the guns still aimed at a forty-five degree to his body scanning for more attackers. Then he hazarded a glance behind him and saw that everyone within a hundred foot radius had stopped and gotten down low when the shooting had started. Seeing no threats, he holstered one gun, performed a magazine change, and was doing the same on the other side when King put a hand on John's arm and pulled him to his feet, his shoes leaving the ground for a second.

"What...?" John looked at Michael, confused.

"I didn't recognize the danger until he had the knife out

and was making his move. I'm sorry," Michael murmured, putting a full mag in his left gun.

Then he pulled some loose rounds from his pouch and started to reload mags as he waited for John to answer.

"That was the slickest kind of cowboy shooting I ever done saw," Tex drawled.

"Sugar, I didn't hardly see you move, and I was looking at you," Caitlin said in awe.

Michael's face burned, but it wasn't embarrassment, it was a shame. He'd been almost too slow, and it could have cost his friend's life. This was the man who'd promised to take care of him when the world went belly up, when he hadn't quite figured out the kind of man he wanted to be. Well, now he had figured it out, and he'd almost failed - and failed badly in his own view.

"You got nothing to apologize for," John said, then coughed into his hand, clearing his throat. "I had no idea he was even coming."

"Kid, you done good, don't you worry none 'bout *'coulda, woulda, shoulda'*. You dig?" King asked.

"I should have seen it earlier. This is exactly what we're trying to prevent from happening," Michael said, his anger taking the place of his embarrassment.

"Kid, you ain't never lost nobody in battle. Sometimes it happens. You do your best and go on. It's a good thing you think you're better than all of us and that you have to protect all of us, but dammit, I'm a fighter, too," King said, shocking them all into silence.

"I didn't say I was better than all of you," Michael protested in a soft voice.

"Then don't assume it's all on you. You did a good job, now quit feeling guilty. You ain't responsible for my safety. You got my back, but at the end of the day, we're all responsible for ourselves. Remember what they say about assumptions?" King asked him, meeting Michael's angry tone of voice with his own.

"That they are the mother of all F-ups?"

"When you assume, you make an ass out of you and me," King said. "Now, unless you want some more PT, let's figure out who this asshole is and we'll..."

King's words trailed off as Shannon and half a dozen men walked up. John held his carbine at the ready, and Michael put his right hand on the butt of the Colt. They hadn't expected so many to be coming back with her, and more than a few of the men there looked mad enough to start shouting Trump at a Hillary Clinton convention. Smith said something into his radio, and the rest of them got ready for what could be a gruesome situation.

"Reporting as ordered, sir," a man with 'Barnes' stenciled on his sweats said, snapping off a salute.

"Agent Barnes," John said, "Agent Shannon Richardson has told us some about you. I suppose you've figured out why we are here?"

"The rumors I've heard, sir, are that your group is to infiltrate this facility, gain access to sensitive data and flush the traitors out into the open," he said, looking at Shannon, who nodded.

"Yes, that's correct. For some time now, the New Caliphate has been receiving high-level leaks from our own government, and were getting resupplied with US Armaments. We discovered that it was elements within your own organization..." Barnes started to respond, and John held up a hand to placate him, "and Sections of the Department of Homeland Security that were working with the New Caliphate. The real tipping point was finding out that the head of DHS, Hassan, went AWOL right before the EMP.

Then he popped up again, *after* it was believed he'd been killed in the small yield nuclear attack on DC. What we're trying to do here, Agent Barnes, is sort through those who were here and those who actively knew of the treason. I have taken this facility by force, but I'm woefully under-staffed, unless I just start lining people up and shooting them."

"You can't do that, the Geneva convention..."

"Oh, I know, they'll be treated in a humane matter. What I need help with, though, is sorting through who we can trust, and isolating the men who were working with the Jihadis," John told him, "preventing lone wolf attacks like that," he said, pointing to the corpse on the floor that had bled all over him.

"How do you know they were working with the New Caliphate? I mean, you could be some right wing extremist group claiming you came in here with the government's blessing and—"

"Sugar, look at this," Caitlin turned the computer around so she could show Barnes and his men - and woman - what she was looking at.

It was a view from a security camera on the third floor. Several bodies littered the floor, where they had fallen after eating the doctored food. Two days of death had given them time to stiffen up and the blood to pool at their extremities. Then Caitlin hit a button and it showed another view with three more bodies out in the hallway, collapsed.

"Who are those people?" one of Barnes' men asked.

"Why are they wearing traditional Muslim garb? That's not regulation," asked another.

"They aren't DHS, not those, at least. Some of their handlers with the DHS ate the tainted food, though. What I need help with..."

John told them, and soon everyone was nodding. Several of the men cracked their knuckles and looked at the DHS agents who were still wearing base's regular uniforms. Then King led them to the armory they had secured, and issued them all batons and side arms after Caitlin had verified everybody's names and ID.

Michael hung back with Shannon whose hand snaked its way into his as they watched them start the rounding up of traitors.

"Do you think this is the end of it?" she asked him.

"No, but it's the beginning of the end."

"Hey, kid," one of the agents who'd been walking with Shannon stopped and turned to face Michael. "Boss might not want to string these guys up, but the rest of us aren't so squeamish. I always was led to believe traitors should be shot by firing squad."

"Right now, I think it's a waste of bullets, and trust me, we're gonna need them all," Michael shot back.

7

"... Are you sure of that? Over," Sandra asked.

"Say again," Sgt. Silverman echoed, "over."

"The President has been assassinated. We're only releasing this information to very tight, need to know group of people. We're in contact with Col. Grady, and we're trying to bring him in. Over."

Blake was holding a sleeping Chris in his arm, over his right shoulder. He'd fallen and twisted his ankle playing with the older kids and wanted some extra cuddles. Blake was more than happy to give it to him, but his recently healed gunshot wound was bugging him, and while most of his strength had come back, not all of his stamina had yet returned and he was running on empty.

"Did I just hear that correctly?" Blake asked as Silverman's transmission finished.

"Shhhh," Sandra chided and waited for the answer, David and Patty turning white as a sheet as they stood beside the large radio setup in Blake's living room.

"I said the President has been assassinated. His top aide Patrick is responsible. He said something to the Secret

Service agent, before he was killed in an escape attempt, to the effect that he made a deal with the Chinese. We think... it was some sort of retaliation, because of the less than strategic nuclear strike on Pyongyang. We had reports of long range Chinese bombers flying over the Pacific, but they turned back before they reached Hawaii. Over."

"What about subs? Over," Sandra asked.

"We've had several tense moments, and we had to command detonate several torpedoes we fired at what we thought were Korean Navy subs. Over."

"Are we still firing on the North Koreans? Over," Sandra asked, her voice barely audible even in the deathly quiet of the house.

Outside, you could hear kids laughing, grownups talking, and the pop of the communal fire as dinner was being prepared and eaten in shifts.

"Yes, ma'am, the holdouts have tried some crude cruise launched missiles on the far east coast, but so far our missile defense system has been more than a match for them - if they don't blow up on launch, that is. Over."

"I can organize the ground war here at home. I've gotten word that the main intelligence element of the New Caliphate has been captured or killed, but organizing a campaign to protect the air and sea is more than I am capable of. We need Col. Grady to come in. Over."

"That's why we're in contact with you, ma'am. We've requested the Col. to make himself available to help us out, but he told us he would be in touch and we haven't spoken with him yet. We were hoping that you'd speak to him, to tell him how much the country needs him right now. Over."

"I can try. I have his frequency and scrambler codes, but I haven't been in contact with his new location as of yet. Over."

"I have a pretty good idea of where he's at," the airman said with a note in his voice that sounded amused, "but I think he can do what we need him to do from where he's located. If you'd contact him, we'd appreciate it, over."

"Understood, I'll make the call. Over and Out," Sandra said and put down the handset.

Her hand was shaking, and Blake started toward her, but Patty was already sliding a bench under her as Sandra sat down hard. Blake handed Chris off to David who was still silent, and sat on the stool, straddling it and put his arm on his wife's back as she took deep breaths and held her stomach.

"You okay?" Blake asked her.

David slid into place after putting Chris in the recliner and put on the headset so he could continue monitoring communications. He had been a tagalong of a gang that had enslaved women and children and, though he had never committed the crimes himself, he still felt guilty. So while at the Homestead, he had done everything he could to make the suffering less, in small ways. He felt that he'd finally found a home when the ladies had shown him forgiveness and started to make him feel like he fit in.

"Got a little whoopsie feeling," Sandra said. "I can survive the morning sickness fine, but I didn't know being pregnant would make me feel faint."

"Horse puckey," Lisa said, coming up the stairs in a rush. "All this stress isn't good for you or the baby."

"I'm okay, Mom, really," Sandra told her, a smile breaking the frown she'd been wearing, "I just got a little nauseous then my legs felt a little bit rubbery. I'm sitting." Sandra pointed to the bench to prove the point.

"Um, Sandra," David said, holding one ear of his

headset he almost wore religiously now, "we've got John Norton on the horn."

"Is there any problems with the DHS facility? I guess there's no rush to get that computer data to the President now."

"You know, I hadn't thought about that... No, it seems that somebody John knows has recently surfaced. John said he doesn't play well with others, but he's a mad dog type of unconventional warfare expert. He sent this man to our contacts in El Paso."

"Who is it?" Sandra asked.

She waited while David talked back and forth with John, "He goes by Mike, was friends with Dick Pershing and—"

"Oh shit, I thought he was dead," Sandra said, then put her hand over her mouth and looked to where Chris was sleeping.

Blake rubbed her arms as her whole body broke out in goose flesh.

"Who is he, hun?" Blake asked.

"King knows him better than me," Sandra said, "he trained him. Mike... is a complicated guy. He's definitely somebody you want on your side, as long as there are sides to draw."

"What do you mean complicated?" Lisa asked, sitting next to her, fully intending to make sure Sandra wasn't overly stressing herself out.

"He worked with small teams. He was the lone survivor of an ambush that killed his best friend. After healing, he wasn't the same. Some people say he had severe PTSD, some said he was a functioning psychopath, and a lot of people thought that if there was something impossible to do, you called in Mike. Hell, I don't even know if Mike is his real name. It changed over the years like mine did, but you can always tell by his face. He never changed that. I don't even know how much I know about him is real, rumor, or misinformation."

"What's complicated about that? Besides the last part?" Lisa asked, knowing it was important.

"He was later captured by the Taliban and tortured for almost six weeks when he went UNORDIR and—"

"What's UNORDIR?" Blake interrupted.

"Unless Otherwise Directed, basically saying I'm going here to kill bad guys, have the message delivered while the mission is in progress, and radio silence is absolute. A tricky way to cover his butt... but the torture... we found out about him because there was a large fire in a village on the edge of Pakistan that our intelligence folks were alarmed about. They sent in some spy drones and, walking out of the village, mostly dead, was Mike. They tried to debrief him, but his mind... he snapped. They say everybody has a breaking point under torture and, as far as they could tell, Mike hadn't hit that point yet, but instead he went insane with the drugs and brainwashing they'd tried on him."

"What happened to the people in the village?" Lisa asked, fearing the worst.

"The women and children had fled long before the Taliban took over, but everybody we found had a knife or gun in hand. There were no survivors. I think they said it took six months to get him stable. He was discharged and put on watch, but we all knew that he should have stayed longer. I heard through the grapevine he died of an overdose."

"He's a druggie?" Blake asked.

"Was," Sandra said, "I don't know if he is now. They got him hooked on some pretty rough stuff in 'stan when they were torturing and trying to brainwash him."

"How are you sure this Mike is the same man?" Blake asked.

"If it's Dick Pershing's friend Mike, I heard about him from King between missions. He's one of those ghosts of the special ops world that you hope to never meet in a dark alley."

"How much of a badass does he have to be to scare you?" Patty asked.

"It's not so much he's a badass, but more like he's a force of nature. He has luck in bucket loads and has no problems throwing himself in harm's way. The missions almost always look like suicide runs, but he kept not dying... I don't know how much of his mind is left, but if he's back in the picture, we could use him, just... not here. Not in Kentucky."

Blake shifted uneasily. He knew how scary and revered his wife was, just by what was said by other people. Knowing there was somebody out there who gave *her* the willies... he almost broke out into goose bumps himself. He knew she was one of the most respected and feared in the spec ops community, but this Mike guy sounded unhinged and like a loose cannon. Blake wasn't going to disagree with his wife's word. Not here in Kentucky.

"Well, he's heading to El Paso," David said. "John wanted to know how much you want to read him in on, and if it was fine to get him secure comms. He told Mike he would, but now he's having some second thoughts."

"Mike would never betray the country *or* a friend," Sandra said immediately. "I'm not worried about him having access to our network of people. Tell him to go ahead and give Mike whatever it is he needs."

"What target do you want him to focus on? That's the second part of John's question," David said, and then mumbled 'wait one,' into the handset mic.

"I'd love for him to take out the cartel that's keeping the central supply lines somewhat working."

"The cartel? One man?" Blake asked.

"I don't know whether or not he's alone, but he graduated King's school of dirty tricks in making things go boom. I would imagine he knows a thing or two about traps and force multipliers..." A grin broke out on her face.

"Part of you wants in on that fight," Blake stated.

"Yes," she admitted, "but the operations part. I'm... not the same woman I was a few years ago."

She got up and headed toward the bedroom and Blake followed. David got busy talking with John, knowing enough about coordinating things to not need to bug Sandra. As the militia was activated and organized, each unit operated much like an independent cell with Sandra and regional commanders as the organizing point of contact.

"What do you think?" Lisa whispered to Patty.

"I think Sandra is right, not in Kentucky," Patty whispered back before turning to put on her headphones.

Lisa walked over to Chris and made him a little more comfortable. She was pulling a throw blanket down to cover him when Blake walked out.

"I was just coming to get him, Mom," Blake said.

"Oh, I was just going to let him sleep there," Lisa said. "I can stay out here and watch him."

Blake hesitated a second and then nodded. "I'm going to sit with Sandra. She has one more radio call to make, and then I'm making her take a break and get some rest. I'm... Mom... she's..."

"She'll be fine," Lisa told him.

"Thanks," Blake said and hugged her hard.

8

Somewhere on the far side of Van Horn, in a run-down gas station that had been abandoned long before the EMP, Mike and Courtney found a US road atlas they could work with. They weren't far from the location when they were able to zero in on the GPS coordinates more accurately. They drove, knowing they were getting close. Fort Hancock, Texas. The GPS coordinates matched the area right on the Mexico/USA border.

The map showed the Mexican side of the border built up like the American side, across the Rio Grande. Once they'd left the major city area, the highways had been very clear. West Texas was hot and very, very lonely. They had passed survivors on I-10, some working on gardens in the ripped up lawns, some herding by hand various cattle. One of the things Mike and Courtney noticed, though, that once out of the big cities, there were more survivors.

Courtney had been driving, and grinned when Mike complained for the thousandth time about her hitting every pothole on the highway. She swerved to hit another one, and Mike cursed while looking at the map.

"Come on," he told her, "we're less than an hour out, and I'm trying to figure out—"

"Dick - Mike!" Courtney shouted.

Mike looked up sharply at her tone. Three men holding AK-47s to their shoulders were blocking the highway.

"Over, under, around or through?" Courtney asked.

"This thing is armored with solid rubber tires. It's half the reason why you haven't busted an..."

Courtney swerved and hit another bump, but this time it was because of muzzle flashes and the sparks that kicked up from the hood.

"Over and through!" Courtney yelled, stomping on the gas pedal.

The diesel engine roared, and the Hummer lurched forward as it rolled even faster. Both of them could hear the gunfire as they roared past the first man in a staggered line. The second jumped out of the way, and the third tried but was clipped by the fender and thrown almost boneless to the side.

"Do you want me to stop?" Courtney asked, looking over her shoulder, and already hitting the brakes.

"It's not the smartest thing in the world, but yeah," Mike panted, reaching for the M4 carbine instead of his beloved KSG.

"Good, cuz I'm gonna... hey, that's my gun," she complained.

She rolled the Hummer to a stop, angling the driver's side toward the left lane sharply so Mike would have cover as he got out. He rolled out as gunfire lessened for a second. Looking through the glass, he saw two of the three performing magazine changes, and the third was motionless on the ground. He laid his M4 over the hood and let off three bursts, hitting both before they had finished their reload.

Courtney barreled out of Mike's side and took a low position behind the passenger side tire, holding Mike's KSG 12 gauge in a low ready position.

"Three down," Mike told her, "cover right as we move up on them. I want to see if these are run of the mill dirt bags or who they're with. Cartels or Jihadis..."

"We could just go," Courtney suggested, before raising the shotgun up to her shoulder and rounding the front grill of the Hummer.

"That'd be the smart choice," Mike replied, following half a heartbeat later.

One of the men they had downed was groaning and rolling around a bit. His AK had fallen several feet out of his reach, and he was a mass of crimson where a burst had taken him low in the torso.

"You're getting old," Courtney teased, picking up on the same jibe she'd used previously.

"Hit him," Mike told her.

"Hey," Mike said, kicking the man's boots when he got close.

He was wearing earth tone pants and a checkered shirt, black work boots, and had shockingly pale skin. His dead companion was dressed similarly but was obviously of Latino descent. The third man... Mike didn't look at him long. He was very dead and not a pleasant sight, with bones sticking out of his leg where he was hit by the armored hummer.

The man spoke between gasps and groans. Mike waited, listening to the rapid-fire Spanish.

"What's he saying?" Courtney asked.

"He wants us to take him to a US medic," Mike answered her and then started speaking to him.

Courtney was patient, but she hadn't used her Spanish in years and years and was beyond rusty. She could make out one word in ten if she were lucky.

"Cartel... violence... girls... movement... food..."

The man pressed his stomach, to hold in his insides in, and started crying and shook his head no. Mike spoke again, this time anger in his voice.

"What did you just say?" Courtney asked.

"He's with the cartels, but he won't say if he's been helping the New Caliphate. Since he's got a one-way ticket to hell already, he says to just put him down and be done with it."

"Oh well, I can do more than that," she said with a grin, and aimed the space age-looking shotgun in the man's crotch.

His pants immediately darkened as he lost control of bodily functions and screamed, before starting talking again. She waited for them both to finish.

"And?" Courtney asked.

"I know more than I did before," Mike said with a grin and pulled the trigger, silencing the man's moans and cries.

Blood flew up, but Courtney had been standing back and was missed by the final spray. Mike wiped some off his face before putting a burst into the still man next to the one he'd been interrogating.

"Just in case," he said, and stripped the two men of their AKs and magazines before turning back toward the Hummer.

Courtney ran ahead and jumped into the driver's side. For once, Mike, the man formerly known as Dick, got in without a complaint as she fired up the engine.

"Where to?" she asked, frustrated that he was so tight lipped.

Mike pointed in the direction of the border.

"What about our meeting?" she asked.

"They are holding dozens of women and children as slaves," Mike said, reloading his carbine, and then reached behind him for a gunny sack full of full magazines and ammo.

He topped off his magazine as Courtney went bouncing over the desert and hills.

"MIKE, NORTON'S ON THE RADIO," COURTNEY WHISPERED AS they were getting out.

She and Mike had traded spots after a half hours' worth of driving, once they'd got over the makeshift bridge that had been erected since the EMP.

"Tell him I'll call him back. I need you to stay here—"

"You're not leaving me behind," Courtney said.

"You're not going with me on this one," Mike said. "This is one time I need you to stay out of this fight, unless they come running to you."

"Why?" Courtney asked, angry with her friend.

"Do you remember how I rescued you?" he asked her.

"Yeah, you bluffed your way in and... wait, you're not going in there to kill all the bad guys, are you?"

"No, but if the opportunity shows up, I will. After all the hostages are rescued. I need you to play ears for me on the handset. The cartel here is in tight with the Caliphate, I'm guessing. If I can get the folks out and leave some surprises... you might get a chance to get some more revenge. Probably more so than me."

"You're taking all the risk," Courtney said, still angry.

"In this case, I'm a somewhat tanned, dark salt and pepper-haired guy. I could easily pass as Latino or gringo. You, on the other hand, are blonde haired and blue eyed. The color isn't uncommon in Mexico, but your looks would make anybody suspicious."

"Why is that?" she asked, anger dripping with every word.

"Because in the vacuum of power here, women became commodities, just like what happened to you in Chicago. You're free. It's safer—"

"I don't want to sit back while there are people out there who were like me and need help!" she yelled.

Mike winced, glad the doors were closed, but the windows were down, and the sound could have carried.

"There's only two of us right now," Mike said, "and I need a set of eyes. Yes, I can probably go to the rendezvous point and ask for help, but it's people I don't know and don't trust. It'll also add a few more hours, and neither of us would want to wait that long."

"This bullshit is ridiculous," Courtney said in a softer voice.

"And you've seen me pull off some ridiculous bullshit, haven't you?" Mike asked.

She was silent and then nodded.

"Plus, there's a third reason I want you to stay back."

"Why?" she asked after a moment's hesitation.

"Because you're my friend, and I wouldn't trust anybody else to go back to Arkansas for me if I don't make it back from this."

"Dammit, Dick... Mike... you don't have to—"

"Yes, I do. We're half a mile from the old church they are operating out of. When the time is right, I want you to contact Norton and his people and give them the heads up, in case I flush some bad guys north across the border."

Courtney pulled off the headset and lurched across the middle of the Hummer and pulled him into a tight hug. He held back a second and then hugged her back.

"I'm keeping the KSG for now, and you're taking extra goodies," Courtney said.

"Yes, ma'am. And... I'm taking all of the C4 we got from the mining office in Texarkana.

"All of it?" Courtney asked.

"Well, a lot of it," he said with a grin. "I might want to leave some surprises and traps. First, though, I have to figure out if the guy was telling me the truth or not."

"I hope it was all a lie, I hope there are no hostages."

"I'll be in touch every hour. You know which frequency to monitor. I'll hit the transmit button every so often so you know I'm still kicking. Don't transmit back unless it's urgent."

"I can't believe you're making me stay back here," Courtney said, her voice devoid of anger.

"You'll get your chance at revenge. After we've freed the hostages."

"How are you going to get them out of there?" she asked.

"I'll improvise," he told her, and opened the door.

9

"How many are left?" King asked.

"Missing three," Michael said.

"Is that including level three?"

"Yes," Tex said, wincing as he shifted to his left leg a bit.

"Then I want pictures printed of those three, and we're going to do a roll call of everyone. If we can't find them that way, I want every parked piece of armor searched. Smith has to pull out and reposition for something Sandra has cooking, and I want the last of the regular DHS Jihadis found before we're left short-handed."

"Don't forget, the former DHS who weren't with them are working with us now," Michael said, trying to be helpful.

"Yeah, Hun," Shannon said, looping an arm around his waist, "but we can't trust everybody. This is just what we now know about this base and facility."

"She's right," King said, pointing to her and giving her a smile.

Shannon slid slightly behind Michael unconsciously, and the big man noticed and flashed her a toothy grin. When King smiled, it reminded a person how much a guy his size needed to eat to maintain his bulk of muscle and sinew, and Shannon was more than a little intimidated by the big man that radiated good health and physical power.

"Ok. It makes sense. Let's get her boss in on it, though. When's Smith pulling out?" Michael asked.

"An hour ago," John told him, "I just wish I'd gotten Mike on the horn before he did. He hasn't shown up at the drop point."

"What do you need Mike for?" Caitlin asked, sitting on one of the bottom bunks in the block they had been sleeping in.

"He's about to go to war down south, at least that's the word I got from Sandra, and has been passed to our contacts in El Paso. They want a way to break into the New Caliphate's communications, and the Mexican Cartel connection has been deemed the easiest way."

"He'll check in," Tex said, "gotta have faith. Now, let's go have a look see for these fellows who have gone missing."

"What do we do when we find them?" Michael asked.

"Well, we can't keep feeding and watching all of our prisoners, so we're gonna have to turn them in, let them go... or..."

"Sugar, don't make the words out loud," Caitlin said before he could finish his thought.

"Nobody turning them loose," King said, his smile from earlier gone, "They knowingly went off the reservation. They will have a court martial to decide their fate. I'm sure we can find somebody here."

"What if it means a firing squad?" Michael asked, and then winced as Shannon poked him in the ribs hard.

"They are traitors, and this is war," King said simply and stood, the bed moving noticeably when his weight was removed. "I don't like it either, but that's law. Law doesn't say it has to be us doing the deed."

SHANNON AND MICHAEL WERE HOLDING A SHEET OF PAPER with the three images and profiles for the unaccounted for DHS agents.

• Melinda Bates –

Age: 42, Agent with DHS for the last five years. Formerly of the ATF. Widowed on 9/11/2001 when the twin towers came down.

• Paul O'Brien –

Age: 54, Senior Agent and Base Commander. Formerly Cia Analyst and Formerly ATF.

• Carl Bates –

Age: 27, Agent of DHS. Language specialist. Formerly ATF.

NEITHER OF THEM RECOGNIZED ANY OF THE AGENTS, AND what they had been finding was that for the most part, the agents who were in the treasonous plot had largely kept to themselves with the exception of the guards topside, the kitchen staff, and the medics. When the evacuation had forced everyone out, it had been pretty easy to figure out who was who by the uniforms, but not everyone evacuated in uniform.

When Caitlin had wiped the computer to prevent the rogue DHS from bringing it back online, it had contained the information that had been saved by all the new agents who were sheltering in place until further orders. Her wipe erased that portion, and when she re-created the server's disk image, it was a revision that didn't have that. That was why they were walking around the facility with a dozen other agents of the Kentucky Mafia looking for the three who were unaccounted for. Michael was armed, and Shannon had been given a carbine to use while she was working with them.

Both were wary, and many of the DHS Agents looked at the group holding the facility on lockdown with either awe or mistrust. They had been given information, but they had no way to verify it, just that they'd been ordered to stand down and many of them had been attacked by groups for one reason or another. It wasn't that the agents not involved in the treason were innocent, but they were innocent of that particular crime. There were agents there who had worked with FEMA and with some camps, while other groups, like Shannon's, had been doing work with ICE or the DEA.

"Excuse me," an agent clad in the same sweats that everyone had been issued approached them.

He was in his early thirties, slim built, but with a military-style haircut and a jagged scar that ran down his right cheek from his ear to his chin.

"Yes?" Michael asked, stopping, the printed sheet in his left hand to leave his more dominant hand free should things go south.

"I, uh... This is going to sound bad, but we've heard on the shortwave that the President has been assassinated."

"What?" Shannon asked.

"I don't know anything about that," Michael said, "I thought we were in a communications blackout?"

Which was true for the DHS, but not the Kentucky Mafia.

"Well, see, a few of us have a small handheld set, and there's rumors flying around on some of the higher bands.

Me and some of my guys were wondering, if that's true, are we free to go soon?"

"I don't know," Michael admitted, "I haven't heard anything myself, and my buddies are pretty plugged in, all the way to the White House. You know why the stand down order was issued?"

"No, sir, I just know when things went south, y'all seized power and rounded up a small amount of people. A lot of people at first thought you were terrorists, but there's been rumors that you were sent in here acting as counter terror operations."

"Yeah," Shannon said, "they were tasked with getting in here and disabling and capturing the agents who were working with the New Caliphate."

"Traitors," Michael said.

The man looked at them and then gave them a nod, "So you're just sorting through who's who?"

"Yes, actually, and there's three agents left. Depending on the orders we get, once we find these three, there will probably be some debriefing/interrogations before we make a determination of when people should be dismissed, or where they will be reassigned," Michael told him simply, echoing something John had mentioned.

"You're awful young to be doing this kind of work, aren't ya?" the agent asked.

"Yes, it was more of a necessity than choice, if you know what I mean."

The agent grinned, and Shannon put a comforting hand on the back of Michael's belt, but she was careful to stay out of his arm's way in case Michael needed to move. Her own carbine was slung over her shoulder, so if something happened, it would be up to Michael to make a move first.

"I suppose since the EMP, there's been a lot of that. Who all are ya looking for?"

"These three," Michael said, handing the man the sheet.

The agent studied it a moment, then his hand went up to scratch the scar. A nervous habit if Michael had to guess, but the man's eyes widened and he handed the sheet back to him.

"They're in the sick bay, the medical... you know? They are patients."

"Are you sure?" Shannon asked.

"Yeah, I've been helping out with cleanup and laundry services. Being stuck in here with no job to do makes me jumpy. I'm used to having something to do, anything. That's what drove me crazy about the Army, hurry up and wait... so when my time was up, I applied to—"

"Thanks, I appreciate it," Michael told him.

The agent nodded and started to walk. They both watched, to make sure he wasn't going to go running to medical, but instead he headed toward the mess hall.

"Want me to call it in?" Shannon asked, pulling out her handheld.

"Yeah, get King and John on the horn," Michael told her quietly, his voice almost lost to the sound of humanity.

"You going to wait for them?" Shannon asked, following as Michael started to stride forward purposefully.

"No, I don't think we have time. They've been here in plain sight all along," he said over his shoulder.

Michael didn't mean to leave her in his wake, he thought she was right behind him but somebody bumped into her, and she turned to apologize, and when she turned back he was gone. She hurried after him, but with everyone from all floors stuck on the top level, it was crowded, and many folks were sharing the beds and sleeping in shifts. Still, there were a lot of people around.

Michael strode into medical to find that it was half full of people. The senior doctors had been ordered to stay and work, but they were under guard by Tex.

"What's going on, kid?" Tex asked.

"They're here," he said, smacking the sheet to his chest as he walked past him and around the counter where the secretary/receptionist/scheduler was at.

"Excuse me, the doctors are seeing a patient—", she started to say.

"Out of my way," Michael told her coldly.

She tried to get in front of him with an angry frown, and he paused half a second to draw his Colt and put it under her chin. Her eyes went wide.

"Tex, show her the picture and ask her what room they are in. If she so much as even speaks anything but that room number, I'm going to redecorate the walls," Michael said coldly.

Tex walked up behind him, his carbine in one hand, and he held up the sheet of paper Michael had passed to him.

"Four," she said quietly.

"Room four, all of them?" Michael asked, his eyes boring into hers.

"Yes," she whispered.

"Sit down." He motioned with the gun.

She did, and Tex fished in his pocket and found two large zip ties. He fastened each wrist to the chair and then followed as Michael went back to the patient care rooms. They both knew from the files there were two doctors, and Michael figured he'd slow things up a bit.

"You want to take the lead?" Michael asked.

"Yeah, considering I know the layout. You cover me. Door swings left, I go left, you go right," Tex said.

"Got it, but, Tex?"

"Yeah?"

"I only see three patient rooms," Michael said as Shannon ran into the room, almost out of breath.

"King, John, and the rest..." she paused and took a deep gulp of air and saw the bound receptionist who was now silent and looking like she was ready to soil her pants, "...on their way. There's too many people to move fast..." gulp of air, "so I had to run around the outer edge."

"Girlfriend there," Michael said pointing to the receptionist, "says that the three agents are behind door number four."

"So let's bust in and arrest them," Shannon said directly.

"There's no number four, just the three patient rooms and the staff bathroom..." Tex said, pointing at the four doors in the short hallway behind the reception desk.

Michael stiffened and nodded.

Tex walked over to it and jiggled the handle to see if it was locked. It was, so he stood to the side.

"Where's the keys?" Shannon asked.

"The doc—"

Her words were interrupted as door two opened and a doc walked out, running into Michael, smacking his face on Michael's forehead. Michael pushed the doc back hard, and he went sprawling on his ass as he slid across the commercial tile floor.

"What's the meaning of..." his words trailed off as Michael showed him his Colt.

"Where're the keys to room four?" he asked.

"I don't know what you're—"

"Don't jack around with this one, doc," Tex said. "He's

too young and hot-headed. Just give him the keys and you and your patient..."

Another door opened, and the other doc poked his head out. Michael drew the other Colt and was covering both docs in a move you only saw in movies.

"Do you have the keys to room four?" Michael asked.

"I told you, he's got a temper and his gun's likely to—"

Michael fired off one shot. It startled everyone but Tex who had seen the young man wink at him. The waiting room of the medical clinic started to empty, and people screamed. A man ran out past the doctor from one room, still wearing a paper robe, and a woman screamed behind door number two, where he had knocked the doc on his ass.

"Patient's out," Shannon yelled, her voice wobbling.

They ran, but when the doc on Michael's left went to move, he lowered the pistol so the next shot wouldn't go cleanly over his head. Shannon advanced to where she was standing in front of Michael, though the doctor never looked at her. She almost brought up the point it was misogynistic to dismiss a woman with a loaded gun as a threat, but she held her tongue.

"This is... you can't... I didn't..."

"Give me the keys to room four, or I'm going to start shooting the lock off and maybe hit whoever's hiding back there."

"You can't do that, the law says..."

The doc on the left took another two steps toward Michael, probably figuring on attacking what he thought was the weaker arm, but before he moved, Shannon made her own play. She reversed the grip on her carbine as she was swinging. Michael swung both guns at the doc and her swing connected with the doc just as he was putting tension on the triggers. Michael let up and took a step to his right as the doc crumpled, his wind knocked out of him from where he'd been stroked in the sternum.

"You don't wanna keep playing games with these young fellers," Tex said calmly to doc number two and raised his own carbine. "Now give me the keys before I let these two start using you for a punching bag, or worse."

He was beyond the point of speech, and he reached into his pocket and came out with two keychains. After looking at them for a second, he tossed one to Tex, who caught it with one hand and held it up. A single key dangled from a lucky rabbit's foot keychain.

"Well, isn't that special?" he asked with a grin.

10

The retired marine known as Mike, and formerly Dick Pershing, approached the old church with more than a healthy bit of caution. It had been disgustingly easy to penetrate the cartel's perimeter. The men were well armed and, by the look of things, their Jihadi buddies had brought some toys with them. They all had newer AK-47s or AK-74s, he couldn't tell from the distance, but they had a very loose kind of discipline. They never altered their perimeter walks, there was no noise or light discipline in the waning light, and they often called out loud to each other.

The one thing he hadn't seen yet was evidence of hostages being held, just some heavily armed cartel bully boys. Mike used the growing shadows once he'd memorized the never changing pattern of the patrols, using parked or disabled vehicles for cover. He'd gotten close to a small fuel tank that had probably started life as an agricultural fuel system for a local farm and put a package there. He checked his watch. Five more minutes till that one went up and then the rest he'd been putting around the compound would go off.

Hopefully, it would provide enough cover and cut down numbers a little bit. Mike didn't have any problem getting rid of bad guys, and from what he could see, these were dressed the same way as the three banditos who'd taken pot shots at them in the Hummer, and they were in the location the dying man had told them about. That was when Murphy of Murphy's Law decided to step on Mike's toes, literally.

Dick was crouching next to a vehicle he'd put a package of C4 and a timer on and knew he had forty seconds until the chain of events started, when a big, bronzed man walked around the corner, quiet as a cat, and stepped on Mike's foot. He almost moved but the man seemed to not have noticed and, to be fair, the concrete and asphalt of the church's parking lot were mostly gone, with deep potholes and chunks sticking up here and there.

The man unzipped his fly and was about to let loose his bladder, when Mike pulled his foot back, making him stumble forward a bit. He grabbed him by the hair and, before he could make a shout, he raked his KaBar across his throat before yanking him down. The loudest sound was the man hitting the ground and his AK clattering to the concrete while the man feebly tried to kick and hold the blood in with his hands.

"Ernesto?" the man on patrol called from twenty feet away.

"Don't have time for this," Mike whispered to himself, checked to make sure his carbine was ready, and did a last second pat down on his tactical vest almost out of habit before moving out of a crouch.

He made it thirty feet to behind a row of broken down cars. The windows had been beaten out, a lot of the sheet metal parts removed, and what was left of the engine was mostly the block. These cars didn't have inflated tires, and he'd mentally planned on using them for cover when the bombs went off, but at the last second, he was spotted by the patrolman who shouted as he slid in.

"Time to improvise," he said, and then closed his eyes and opened his mouth.

The first explosion almost sounded like a monstrous heartbeat, but it was two explosions. The charge had ruptured the fuel tank, and the fumes and gasoline inside made a much larger blast than the small package of C4 he'd used there. The pressure wave was enormous, and despite his closed eyes, the sun down was lit up like a demonic Molotov cocktail. He waited two seconds and looked up over the side of the hoodless car as shouts lit the air. The first target he saw was the man who had been walking the patrol.

"Boom," Mike said as he was running past the next car that was ready to go.

It went up in flames, the explosion nothing like the one the gas vapors had ignited, but it was large enough to lift the car and throw it on its side, right on top of the cartel member. His shouting turned into screeches for a second, and then stopped. Like kicking a wasp nest, cartel members boiled out of the church, guns raised. But they were looking in the wrong direction, and it cost them.

The next car exploded, this one a shiny low rider that was obviously somebody's pride and joy. As that went up, Mike put three bursts down range, cutting down cartel members in the back of the bunched up group. They scattered toward Mike, and he held his position another few seconds until the next car exploded, hitting the bulk of the group with the flash and shrapnel. This had been an older Buick or Oldsmobile; its hood, doors, and glass were gone, but the engine on it shone as if it had just been installed.

Not any more, the motor flew a good ten feet past the body.

Mike started to run for the church. His goal was the concrete steps leading up to the front door. It was time to get out of dodge as the last two explosions were imminent and he was too close. He took off running as the group saw him. They opened fire immediately. He couldn't see how many were left standing, nor pick it out over the screams, shouts, flames and the pop and crackle of flesh as the dead were still too close to the fire.

A round hit him square in the back, right on the plate, and he was thrown on his face, losing a yard of his cheek and neck until his momentum was spent. The slide did another thing that saved his life as rounds kicked up dirt and rocks near him... he slid in next to the concrete steps. Again, he closed his eyes and made sure to open his mouth as another car went up. He didn't open his eyes until the last explosion went off and then he tried to turn over.

His back felt shattered, broken. His legs didn't want to work, so he focused on blocking out the pain and wiggling his toes. He felt them scrape his sock against the toe of the boot. Not having time to be incapacitated with pain, he pulled himself up to his knees using the side of the steps, his carbine and elbow on one side, his hand on the other. A man was walking through the wreckage, a pistol in his hand and both hands to the side of his head. He was stalking back and forth between the dead, screaming incoherent words. Mike took careful aim and put three rounds down range and watched the impact. The man spun toward him in slow motion and aimed his pistol in Mike's direction.

The man fell about the same time Mike was able to get his left foot up and on solid ground. He powered up and got to his feet slowly, and put his back to the outer wall of the church, breathing in deeply. It was a lot closer than he'd expected. He did a quick mag change for a full one, putting the half fired one in his dump pouch. The ring of fire and black smoke from burning cars and fuel was like something out of Dante's Inferno. The screams had died off, but the flames still licked the air hungrily. A sickly sweet smell of cooking meat reached his nose, and he fought off the gagging sensation.

All targets down. He hadn't gotten a count, but he could see twelve forms, or what he thought were the torsos of twelve forms. That was when he realized he was hearing something from within the church. It wasn't yelling but crying. A different pitch than the shouts and screams of men. Higher pitched, softer, yet with volume. Feminine. Mike eased around the corner and walked up the steps and looked in the glass pane of the front door. The frosted glass was hard to make out the interior, it was dark inside, and the reflection of the fires behind him further blinded him.

He stood off to the side and pulled the door open wide and made sure to pull back quick. No gunfire followed, but the wailing was more apparent now as he walked in, trying not to silhouette himself. Movement caught his eye, and he turned as the short entranceway opened up to a one room church. The pews had been shoved off to the right-hand side from the doorway, many of them haphazardly thrown one on top of another. On the left side of the church were numerous forms, huddled together, crying, holding each other.

"Stand up, all of you," Mike intoned deeply, his carbine on the low and ready.

"Americano?" a woman called back in a steady voice.

"Si," Mike answered her back.

A woman stood slowly from the middle of the jam pile

of bodies, gently pushing hands away that were trying to pull her back down.

"How many are you?" Mike asked.

"Many, there were more, but the Caliphate took some for wives."

Mike cursed, and many of the women cried out in terror.

"I'm sorry, ladies, I'm here to help, is there anybody else in here?"

"I have not seen Ernesto Cabrillo, he is the head of this..." she said, motioning around.

"Is Ernesto still tight or in contact with the Caliphate?" Mike asked her.

"No, they moved out last week. We were brought here after they were gone."

Too late. He wanted to curse again, but he didn't want to terrify the women more.

"Ernesto is dead. I think I got all of them, so if you'd like to come with me, I'll take you to friends who can help."

"Where?" a small voice asked, and Dick looked down and saw his daughter Maggie.

"Mags?" he asked.

The girl looked at him in confusion, and he walked toward her slowly, watching her, and handed his carbine to the woman he'd been talking to. She hesitated and then pointed the carbine at him, its barrel shaking.

"Don't do it, Mary," Dick told her, "that's the end you fire from. You know how to shoot, we spent a ton of time at your dad's farm, I'm just getting—"

"Mister?" the little girl said, holding her arms out.

He lifted her and Mary finally lowered the barrel. She spoke in rapid-fire Spanish, and the rest of the women moved apart slowly. Dick heard one of them mutter 'loco' but ignored it as he put the little girl back down. It wasn't his daughter, he'd done it again. He'd slipped. In the heat of combat, he was laser focused, but in the aftermath, his mind reverted to the psychosis that had ruled over him the last four years. Having gotten a dose of the real Maggie and Mary, he was able to fight off the delusion with some effort.

"I'm sorry if I scared you, you looked like my daughter; I got a little confused," he said to her.

"Is okay, mister. Where are we going?"

"Over the river," Mike said, fighting back the darkness that had consumed much of his life.

"That is where we were heading when we were captured," the woman he called Mary said and, after a moment, she held up the carbine, stock up.

Mike took it and slung it over his shoulder.

"How did you know my name was Mary?" she asked, her accent thick.

Mike ignored her question. "Who needs help? Is anybody hurt?"

11

"He did it," Sandra said with a grin.

"Who did what?" Blake asked, lying in bed with his wife.

Neither of them could sleep, and Chris was crashed out on his toddler bed in the corner of the bedroom. With the Homestead not being as densely populated now, there was room for him to take a room in the basement, but he preferred to be with his adopted parents. Blake didn't mind; the horrors the kid had seen probably haunted him the same way as Sandra, who tossed and turned, calling out names of the dead.

"Mike. Information was spotty, but apparently, he just staggered into camp with his companion, Courtney, and about twenty women and young girls. He hit the cartel."

"Is everyone okay?" Blake asked.

He knew his wife had gone to the other room for that transmission, and he'd figured it was because she was restless and didn't want to wake him or Chris.

"He's got road rash, but they patched him up and shot him full of antibiotics. The ladies..." Sandra made an iffy gesture with her hand, "...they were hurt pretty bad, half of them have STDs from their ordeal. They are doing what they can but... there's one lady who's in pretty bad shape."

"How did he do it?" Blake asked her.

"They don't know. He managed to get everyone back to Courtney with a stolen farm truck, and then once they made the meet he kind of fell apart."

"What do you mean?" Blake asked her.

"He kept demanding to see his daughter Maggie. It took so long because Courtney had to take him to a dark room in an abandoned house near the meet-up to sit on him to get him calm enough to debrief."

"He's a loose cannon," Blake said, his skin breaking out into goose bumps.

"He's on our side, though," she said. "There's a lot of people like him in the world. Damaged by what they've gone through, what they were forced to do. That might make some of them scary, but it's not really their fault," Sandra said, her nail scratching across Blake's stomach until he twisted as it tickled.

"Stop," Blake said, turning to her with a grin. "So it was a success?"

"Yes, he even got the cartel boss, but the Caliphate contacts had already moved out."

"I wonder why?" he asked rhetorically.

"Well, remember one of our goals was for him to get some communications gear from them?"

"Yeah?"

Sandra turned on her side to face him. "He got it. They are building up division strength groups. Sounds like John's group was wildly successful, and we have DHS traitors who are singing like canaries. It'll all be over soon."

"How so?" Blake asked.

"As soon as Col. Grady gets to a secure location, I'm going to pass the locations of the massed troops to him for the Air Force to do a bombing run. This war for America... If it turns out they really are bunched up as they seem..."

"What about collateral damage? What if they have hostages with them? Women they've—"

"I'm not going to make that call, and neither are you," Sandra said, kissing his chin. "I'm going to hand this mess off as soon as I can, and we can go on and raise our kids. It won't be long, and we'll have the farm mostly to ourselves."

"Except for Mom and Dad, Bobby..."

"I know you, Blake, you aren't booting anybody who doesn't want to go. This doesn't need to be a military installation soon. Oh, we'll still have stuff here, but if most of the fight is over, we can reassign a lot of the armor and anti-aircraft systems to Silverman."

"I don't mind having people around," Blake said with a grin, using his finger to trace around his wife's forehead. "I actually like having all the kids around. We've got a pretty good group."

"Yeah, and Keeley is going to mother hen all of the younger ones. I worry she's taking on too much," Sandra said, changing the subject.

"She's doing it to cope," Blake told her. "We had a long talk. She had to be a parent for a sibling when her parents never came home. She was alone when the EMP hit, babysitting. Things were good for a while, but she ran out of insulin for her little—"

"Shhhhh, no more," Sandra said, putting a finger to his lips.

Blake was doing his daily walk with the kids. It was late fall, and it had gotten cold enough to put frost on the ground on some of the hills they wandered. Scavenging teams were looking for winter gear for the growing kids, but more than half of them were already outfitted with years' worth of supplies. Chris was carrying a sack of gleaned goodies for the supper pot when he nudged his father and pointed. Blake looked, and it took him a second. A doe was standing perfectly still, almost eighty yards away. He made a hand motion, and the kids lowered themselves to the ground silently.

Blake made a watch and stay here gesture and stalked forward. The wind was on his back, blowing toward the deer, so he knew he didn't have long to make his shot. The deer had heard their approach and held still, relying on its natural camouflage to keep it hidden. Blake was moving for a better angle for his shot; he had been teaching the kids how to forage and hunt, and he was proud that his son had been the first to spot the deer, even before his father. He stopped behind an old, gnarly tree and took careful aim.

The shot went off, startling Blake as it should have, and he saw the deer hop straight up, half spinning in the air. He worked the bolt on his rifle, and the deer took one bound before its legs folded as it landed.

"You got it," Chris screamed, running up jump tackling his dad in a massive hug.

Blake had put his rifle on safety and raised it over his head as the other kids got up, though not quite as fast nor as enthusiastically as Chris.

"Easy, buddy, I still have a gun in my hands. I put it on safe, but you can't do that, not when we're hunting."

Little hands gave one last squeeze to his waist and then fell away.

"Sorry, Dad, I didn't mean..."

"No harm, no foul. Now we're going to wait a good ten minutes or more before we walk up on it," Blake said.

"Why are we going to wait?" Keeley asked.

"To make sure he's dead. Even if he's dead, his nerves can fire off, making them kick, and they've got sharp hooves. Don't want to get a hole in your head, do ya?" Blake asked her with a grin.

Keeley stood there a moment and put her hand on her hip in a move that reminded Blake of Sandra. "It won't hurt the likes of Jason, he's got nothing up there," she snarked, looking at the teenager.

"When the wind blows hard, your brains get scrambled. We're just lucky that this deer didn't smell you this time."

"I took a bath," Keeley said in a dangerous tone.

"Could have fooled me," Jason told her and bolted.

Blake watched him get four steps before Keeley tackled him. Both were in their mid-teens and were wrestling. What Keeley lacked in size and strength, she made up for in technique and skill and soon had him pinned to the ground, an arm across his throat until he let out a squeak of surprise.

"Maybe she wants to play Legos?" Chris whispered at his grinning dad.

"I do not stink," Keeley seethed.

Jason looked around, and when Blake's eyes met his, Blake shrugged his shoulders to let him know he had this one on his own.

"You don't stink—"

He made a choking sound as she put more pressure on his throat. Blake was almost ready to stop things when she let up.

"What was that again?" Keeley asked sweetly, but

everyone could hear the malice in her words as she strad-
dled him.

"It's just that... when you're around, I can't think right. I
say stupid things I don't mean. I'm sorry."

Keeley looked at him a moment and then pulled her
arm back. Then she got up and held a hand out to Jason. He
took it, and she helped him to his feet. He was brushing
himself off when she leaned in, took his head between her
hands, and made him look up. She planted a wet one on his
cheek and then laughed delightedly when he started to stut-
ter, his face turning an alarming shade of red.

"Took you long enough," she said to him and then
turned to Blake. "Has it been ten minutes yet?"

"Dad," Chris said before he could answer, tugging on his
hand, "I don't think she wants to just play Legos, just
saying."

12
___

"What do we have?" Col. Grady asked, walking into the hastily put together ready room.

It was in a different bunker location, one not far from where he'd been hiding out. This one had better communications equipment and was plugged into everything. He'd agreed to go back and had been giving orders nonstop until he'd gone inside. It was a blackened room with computer terminals at every seat around an oval-shaped table. Monitors showed up to date satellite images on the screen, and there were dozens of people speaking into headsets. Heads of the Navy, Army, and Air Force were all in attendance.

"Our subs have sunk every North Korean sub and surface ship in American waters in the last three hours, sir," an operator he didn't recognize said.

"Casualties?" Grady asked.

"Sir, we lost two Los Angeles Class..."

"Rescue operations?" Grady asked.

"Underway, sir. Ambassador Lin has been on secure communications, and is waiting to hear from you. He insisted you were the only one he would speak with," a different operator told him.

"Tell him I'll be with him shortly," Grady said and turned to his top Air Force liaison. "We've gotten word from the Kentucky Mafia—"

"Sir, the American Militia," the liaison said with a grin.

"We got word from the Kentucky Mafia," Grady said, also grinning, "that somebody has intercepted some of the New Caliphate's comms equipment and they have up to date data on where the main portion of the enemy is located. Do we have views on satellite?"

An operator hit a few keys, and the view on one of the screens changed. The picture wasn't clear.

"We'll have eyes on site within two minutes, sir."

"Good, I want eyes on them as soon as possible. If this is, in fact, their main forces, I want all the newly recalled bombers scrambled and every available drone in the air."

"We may not have enough operators," another man piped up. "A lot of them were in the base that got—"

"I said every available, whether it's lack of materials or men. I want everyone armed and ready to go. Also, I want to know any intel on civilians who may be a hostage with them. We've gotten word that they've taken the women and children from occupied areas. I don't want to be bombing Americans."

"Sir, intercepted intel is saying that the hostages are in the rearmost of the moving column that's heading to the DHS base being occupied by Militia Special Forces Operatives."

"Good. I want somebody on the horn coordinating ground forces with Kentucky. I want them to become the hammer to our anvil. We're going to crush the New Caliphate between the bombing, the ground forces, and the

Rocky Mountains. We're done playing games, and the Rules of Engagement from the previous administration are at this moment revoked. Kill the enemy. This is a fight for our very lives, freedom, and The American Way."

Somebody in the background let out a rebel yell, and soon clapping could be heard around the room. Grady let it go on for a moment and then held up both hands.

"I know you're all be anxious to get to work but—"

"Sir, I have two satellites on target now," an operator said, and suddenly all screens were filling with both sets of feed.

"Good, make sure our intel is good. You boys know what to do."

13

———

"We waited too long to overrun the facility," Khalid complained to his cousin.

"Nothing is certain, and we shall know within the hour. Praise be to Allah! Have faith, cousin."

The men were riding in a looted Hummer they had taken from one of the many bases they had shelled and overran. They had grown confident with their easy success, but much of their long-range plan had been to use a back-door to disable the nuclear deterrent. What they couldn't take by cunning, they would hammer with brute force.

"Hassan, you talk much of faith and your God. How do you know he hears your prayers?"

"Cousin, I just do. I still have a hard time believing you've lost your faith. It's..."

The men sitting behind him shifted uncomfortably as Khalid turned to face his cousin who was driving. What the leader of the New Caliphate was saying was heresy, and put him on par with some of the very enemies they were fighting against, at least that's the doctrine they'd been taught. Most of them had never actually picked up a copy of the Quran and read it for themselves. Most of them were illiterate, only proficient in the art of war in their home-lands... not theological scholars.

"Yes?"

An explosion rocked the Hummer as a missile hit the vehicle immediately behind them. The back of their lightly armored vehicle was hit by shrapnel, and the pressure wave from it made the rear end kick out like they'd suddenly lost traction on ice. Hassan drove into the swerve.

"What was that?" he yelled.

"I don't kn—"

Just in front of them, a troop carrier was hit by some-thing coming straight down. The last thing Khalid saw before they ran into the flaming wreckage was bodies and appendages being strewn all over.

KHALID CAME TO SLOWLY. EVERY PART OF HIS BODY HURT, AND he was sure he was alive only by some miracle. He was lying on his side, and something sticky was dripping down onto the side of his head. It took three tries to move his left arm up to his temple. It came away bloody. That was when he really took in his surroundings. The Hummer had come to rest on the passenger side. What glass there was had shat-tered, and the smell of diesel fuel was strong and pungent, and Khalid realized that he was hit by another drop of something warm to the side of his face.

He looked to his left, which was straight up in the air, and saw his cousin, Hassan, still strapped into his seatbelt, hanging lifelessly. There was visible shrapnel sticking out of his body, and it was obvious he was quite dead. Blood had settled into the areas of the flesh closest to Hassan, making his body look mottled. He noticed the smell: evacuated bowels, blood, and violated organs. He gagged and struggled with his own straps which were holding him in the seat, probably the only thing that had saved him. He fumbled a moment and freed himself and started through the cracked windshield.

He cut his arms and legs pulling himself back through. There was something wrong with his legs; they tingled, and he didn't have full control, but he could feel as the glass shards bit and scraped. Screaming in agony, he pulled himself through. It wasn't just that the cuts hurt, everything hurt. It felt like he was bruised, concussed, and sliced in every inch of his being. Living hurt.

"We got a live one," a big black man said, walking through the wreckage.

He was easily 350 pounds, a mountain of a man. His voice was low and rumbling, and the M4 carbine he was carrying looked like a play toy, carried in hands that looked like they each could wrap around the gun twice. A boy no older than his early twenties ran up to him, his cheeks thick with stubble. A black haired white woman who could be mistaken for a goddess followed as well. The boy wore twin Colt 1911s, and the woman carried a carbine like the big too.

"I... I demand to be treated as a prisoner of war, in accords with the Geneva Convention," Khalid said in English with a British-sounding accent.

The big man looked at him and then down at the ground near his feet. Khalid looked and saw a severed arm holding an AK-47. He kicked at it, dislodging the arm, and then hooked his toe under the AK and kicked it in Khalid's direction. Khalid crawled forward a step, one hand reaching for the rifle. His hand was unsteady, and after a moment, he pulled it back and painfully got to his feet. He wobbled, and his vision swam. He kicked the rifle back toward the group and almost lost his balance. His hand shot out, grabbing the jagged frame where the windshield had been.

"Who are you?" the young man asked, his hand flexing over his right hip where one of the Colts waited in a low slung holster, much like the gunslingers of old.

"I am Khalid, the Spear of Allah, Sword of the New Caliphate."

"Figures," the big black man said, walking closer.

Khalid looked up and up and up. He noticed the plate carrier vest with grenades, a knife strapped to it for a quick pull, and how little of the broad chest of the giant it covered.

"I demand—"

Khalid's air was cut off as King picked him up by the throat. He immediately tried to break the grip with both hands, but King just held him up higher with one.

"Do we need him for intel?" King asked.

"No, all reports say we've got the whole Caliphate captured or dead. I'm sure there are a couple hundred potential stragglers, but the last two days we've pretty much wiped them out.

Two Days? Khalid thought, *I was dead to the world for two days, and now I'm about to die at the hands of an American Wrestler?*

King swung Khalid and threw him into the damaged hood of the Hummer. His back hit first, igniting every ache and pain in his body. Khalid cried out in pain and fell to his hands and knees. If he were going to die, he would be defiant to the... He tried to spit, and nothing came out. No wonder he was weak. Dehydrated and blood loss. He breathed heavily and then made his way to his feet again.

"I demand to be treated with respect and dignity as any foreign commander. Under the Geneva Convention's—"

Michael's gun hand blurred and he fired once, hitting Khalid in the stomach, right where a belt would cinch his pants up tight. Khalid let out an oomph sound and crumpled.

"Why didn't you finish him?" King asked.

"Missed, drew too fast," Michael lied.

King made a disgusted sound and walked up to Khalid. He palmed the Jihadi's head, and lifted him up until his feet were more or less under him.

"You know who I am?" King asked.

"You are an American, an infidel, one of the Great Satan's minions." His words were hoarse as he choked them out.

King changed his grip to hold Khalid up by the throat, but he didn't put killing pressure on the man's windpipe, just one big, meaty hand that wrapped halfway around the Jihadi's neck.

"I am an American. I am from one of the most enlightened nations on all of God's green Earth. I am a warrior for justice and peace. I've made oaths to honor my country, my flag, and to protect it with everything I have. I am the son of a sharecropper whose only life goal was for his own boy to make a better life for himself than everyone else. I did that, and I'm proud of who I am and what I've done."

Michael and Shannon looked at each other in surprise. When King talked, it was significant. When he monologued, it was epic.

"You, on the other hand, are a pissant, goat-humping, hate-filled, failure to your Allah. We've defeated you, all of you. There is no more North Korea to back you up. China has backed off, so there's no support there. The people you have left in the middle east? As we're identifying the bodies, we're alerting the families. No longer will you wage war against us. We will wipe you out *to a person* if needs be. There is no reason on this Earth why people should put up with such hatred and bigotry as your movement has caused. Oh, and that EMP you set off?"

Khalid looked up and smiled.

King grimaced a smile back at him. "I wish I could do this as many times as lives were lost for your crusade."

"What?" Khalid managed to ask.

King's hand tightened, and he twisted his wrist. There was an audible cracking sound, like breaking ice out of a plastic tray, and he let go. Khalid fell to the pavement, his body limp.

The last thing Khalid had known, was that there was a sharp pain as his neck had snapped and then there was no pain after that. He wanted to move, but his body wasn't responding. No pain, no pain anywhere. Who knew that the cure for pain was a broken neck? Were they going to leave him there—?

A burst from the M4 splattered the rest of Khalid's head against the broken pavement. A contrail of smoke came up from the barrel from Shannon's carbine.

"What was that?" Michael asked her. "He was already dead!"

"Rule number two," Shannon said, "double tap."

"Rule Number Two?" King asked.

"Zombieland," Shannon said, grinning.

"I think I love you," Michael said with a cheesy grin on his face.

14

I t had taken him close to a week to recover from the rescue, and Mike was feeling restless. The shot to the back had been stopped by the AR500 armored plate, but the entire plate had left a bruise, and any movement hurt. That paled in comparison to the road rash along the side of his neck, face, and head. It had scabbed, peeled, and scabbed again. The doc said he would have some terrific scars to impress the ladies unless he could find a plastic surgeon. Courtney told the doc to go to hell, to just get him patched up enough to travel.

The healing would have progressed faster, except being tended to like he was made him flash back. When he'd been hospitalized for the shrapnel, the time he was tortured... and all the memories that had been repressed came flooding back. He had no idea who was friend or foe some days. Courtney had suggested a radio call to Arkansas, and Mary was consulted. She gave them the name and dosage of the medication Mike, formerly known as Dick, was supposed to be on. After refusing pain meds, taking his psych meds and a week's worth of bed rest, he was starting to slowly struggle out of the darkness of his own mind in an old emergency clinic Sandra's people had taken for caring for Mike and the ladies they'd rescued.

"You're never going off on your own again," Courtney said for the thousandth time.

"Yeah, well, we'll see about that," he told her.

"Dammit, Mike, we're supposed to be a team," she said, a big tear trailing down her cheek.

"We are. I've told you a thousand times, that mission was a one-man op. I knew I might get bloody, but you did what you were supposed to, and as a team, we got everyone out. Alive even."

"I should have been there, you wouldn't have gotten shot," she said, her voice softening, and she rubbed her hand against the smooth side of his face.

"I needed you to stay safe to get the women and children away, to call in the cavalry when you did. To know to look for the communications equipment that turned the tide of this war. I hear it was new Chinese high-grade gear the Koreans were using, and it would have taken us weeks to crack the code if we didn't have our own radio setup with scrambler and codes."

"Yes dammit, Mike, it was," she said and sat on the side of the bed.

She looked at him and saw a man who'd willingly give up his life to save strangers, who ran into a fight knowing the odds stacked against him. Somebody who wasn't afraid to die for his cause. For a moment she almost sobbed, remembering her own losses and wondering if she'd ever be so selfless, like Mike. He nodded at her words.

"So, we won," he told her. "You can settle down somewhere, rebuild your life, or you can work with the new American Militia as they rebuild the country."

"What are you going to do?" she asked, her heart breaking as she realized he was talking about a life apart.

"I hear there are two large groups of cannibals. They move into one area, torture and kill and then move on out."

"You're going to go after them?" Courtney asked.

"It's what I do. I realized something, lying here in this bed. Everyone has a purpose in life. Some are called to be doctors, some are called to be priests. Some people are called to write books and poetry. Some people are warriors. I figured out all this beating about the bush, losing my identity only to gain it back... overall, I'm a warrior. I'll always need a battle. I figure there's spots of lawless anarchy and bad stuff that'll need to be taken care of for a long time. I'd rather do good than tilting my lance at windmills."

"Do you want some company?" she asked, knowing he'd say no already.

"I'd love some," he told her, taking her hand in both of his.

15

M arch was every bit as cold as they had expected, and then some. Blake's wood stove never stopped burning and the fire stack in the barracks in the barn simmered as well. People had drifted from the Homestead, except many of the kids without families or older men or women with no family around. They lived, worked, and survived together. School was held, and everyone waited for the big melt that.

A helicopter had been sent out to the Homestead on March 1st, one of many unusual ways for the government to handle a vote. Everyone over the age of 18 was given a simple ballot. Blake had voted for Grady, though he had no problem if it was Hines either. Both had been more than honorable men. In other areas of the country, trucks, railroad cars and smaller airplanes that didn't rely on electronics flew in election teams to the population centers. They stayed in place for a week, their locations broadcast over Rebel Radio.

When the time frame was up, they packed up, drove, flew or rode back to a secure bunker somewhere in the hollers and hills. Sandra's stomach had become so swollen that the small woman looked like a grapefruit that had been overwatered on a hot summer day. Grady had a medical team stationed there at the Homestead, with all the medical and surgical gear needed. It was the least the country could do for the two people who had started the great pushback, even if their start was only finding each other.

Keeley and Jason still bickered, and Chris convinced many people to play Legos and tons of board games with him during the unusually cold winter. Everyone got along. Their preps were wearing a bit thin, but they had given so much food to the people as they left so they wouldn't be burdened with starting all over from scratch.

There were three weddings between Christmas and New Years Eve: David married Corrinne, much to everyone's surprise, and Bobby married Melissa, with her father, Curt's, permission. Then Tex and Caitlin returned to the Homestead and married just as midnight rang in, and Duncan performed the adoption ceremony for Linny and Brett the brat. Everyone was merry. In the first week of the new year, Don and a girl named Zelda, or Z, wandered into the Homestead, and Patty immediately took them both in, having grown fond of Z.

On March 16th, a Thursday, Sandra went into labor, somewhat close to her due date. The Homestead was abuzz, and everyone paused what they were doing to wait and listen for news. The pregnancy had left her bedridden after the battle of the Hammer and Anvil, and although the doctors felt they had her stable and the baby safe, there was still a significant risk, and this might be the only pregnancy Sandra could have if she survived. She prayed, but she was hopeful, and she glowed every time somebody would rub her stomach for luck.

Blake was pacing when he heard the distinctive whump whump whump sound of an approaching Huey. He quit pacing and saw the doctors wipe Sandra's brow.

"Go see who it is," Sandra said and gasped as another contraction hit her, and she moaned in pain.

"I should be here," he told her.

"Go, if they are flying in this weather, it's life or death."

Sandra was right. Blake saw the wind had kicked up a lot over the last couple of hours and snow was falling hard, and being blown off the roofs of the house and barn. He saw the helicopter make a landing on the flat spot near where the ice house was situated. He was torn with indecision, and Sandra tried to turn toward him. The docs shouted for her to hold still.

"Just go," she told him, "I need to know... and Blake?"

"Yeah, baby?"

"When this is over," she said, panting through a contraction, "I want chocolate ice cream, remember, you promised."

"I can do that."

Blake swore to himself over the interruption and walked out, pulling his coat off the hook. He was already wearing his boots, so he opened the door and was surprised to see that four armed soldiers in US Marine uniforms, guns held low, were following close behind Col. Grady and Hines, Governor of Kentucky. Blake smiled, having met Grady once and Hines many times during all the work he'd done with him as former head of FEMA.

"Gentlemen, would you all like to come inside?" he asked through gritted teeth.

"Yes, that would be great. You gentlemen can stay here, we won't be long," Grady said to the four armed escorts.

They walked inside, both men stomping their feet. Blake took off his coat and hung it up and looked to see that David and Patty were about to start up Rebel Radio and tell the world that soon Blake would have some news. Corrinne was sitting next to David on the Bench, and Patty was standing and pacing. Lisa, Duncan, and Bobby were camped out on the sofa with Chris sitting on Melissa's lap, who was on the floor. Everyone looked like they were clutching something with bloodless hands, the tension was so high.

"What is it? You'd interrupt him now?" Lisa asked.

"What's going on, ma'am?" Hines asked.

"My daughter, his wife, is about to give birth!" Duncan roared.

They both shrank away from him a bit; Duncan had lost a tremendous amount of weight, but he was still a formidable guy, a man of God or not. Grady dug around in his coat pocket and pulled out a sheet of paper.

"I need to make an announcement, regarding the election. I thought I would come here to the Homestead and announce it to the world over Rebel Radio, with your permission, of course."

"Of course—"

Sandra let out a scream, and Blake left them standing there and slammed the bedroom door. Everyone in the living room stood as Sandra screamed in pain once more. Then there was a soft cry, then it grew louder. A baby's wail blasted through the house, and everyone smiled. If it could scream, it was alive. The tension eased down several notches, and Duncan tried to stand to have Lisa hold onto his arm, pulling him back down.

"This is Blake's time, they will let you in when they're ready."

Grady looked at Hines who shrugged and then smiled. Grady smiled back. They couldn't have known their timing was bad on an epic scale, but Marine One was sitting outside, waiting on them. The country had waited a week after polling was closed to tally the counts, they could wait another half hour, hour...

Time passed like molasses, and then two of the three doctors came out and headed toward the basement where a makeshift bathroom had been set up for them to use, in Bobby and Weston's old room. They ignored calls for information and pretended not to even hear anything.

"Tonight's episode of Rebel Radio will have one Col. Grady and Governor Hines here with us at the Homestead to announce the next President of the United States of America. There is a lot more going on at the Homestead, so we're delaying the broadcast until we have more news. Over," David said into the mic.

There <u>was</u> immediate feedback and lots of <u>well</u> wishes over the air, but that lasted thirty seconds, and then everyone went back to radio silence to wait and see what it was.

Duncan was beside himself, sick of waiting and was getting to his feet, not letting Lisa make him sit this time when the bedroom door opened again and Blake walked out. Grady had been reading over the piece of paper and then took the microphone from David.

"This is Col. Grady, commander of the US Armed Forces. An election was held two weeks ago, and we're here to introduce to you, the winner, by an almost unanimous vote," he paused, and Hines was grinning ear to ear.

Blake walked to both men, a little bit of blood on his cheek and on his shirt, smiling broadly.

"Is everything okay?" Lisa asked him.

Blake nodded. That was when Grady handed him the sheet of paper he'd been holding. Blake read it, his eyes going from Grady to Hines and back to Grady, who was grinning.

"*I'd like to present to you, the President of the United States of America, Blake Jackson!*" Grady announced.

"He wasn't even on the ballot," Bobby whispered, and somebody kicked him.

"Say something, Blake," Grady said, holding the transmit button down for him.

"*It's a girl,*" Blake said, and then shouted, "*It's a GIRL!*"

=-THE END-=

ABOUT THE AUTHOR

Boyd Craven III was born and raised in Michigan, an avid outdoorsman who's always loved to read and write from a young age. When he isn't working outside on the farm, or chasing a household of kids, he's sitting in his Lazy Boy, typing away.

You can find the rest of Boyd's books on Amazon & Select Book Stores.

boydcraven.com
boyd3@live.com

Printed in the USA
CPSIA information can be obtained
at www.ICGtesting.com
LVHW042333061223
765907LV00041B/1171